UNEXPECTED

DESTINATIONS

UNEXPECTED DESTINATIONS

A NOVELLA

CORA LAINE

an imprint of Nicole Frail Books, LLC
Avoca, Pennsylvania

Attic and Attic Ebooks are imprints of Nicole Frail Books, LLC, with offices located in Avoca, Pennsylvania, USA.

For permission requests, write to permissions@nicolefrailbooks.com. To purchase copies of this book in bulk or to stock in your brick-and-mortar stores, please write to sales@nicolefrailbooks.com. For publicity requests or other inquiries, or to get in touch with the author or publisher, write to info@nicolefrailbooks.com.

Cover design by Brooke Gilbert
Section break palm trees by Clker-Free-Vector-Images/Canva
Chapter header palm tree by Demibara/Canva
Edited & Typeset by Nicole Frail/Nicole Frail Edits, LLC.
First publication: August 2025

Learn more about the publisher at:
www.nicolefrailbooks.com | @nicolefrailbooks
www.attic-ebooks.com | @attic.ebooks
www.andyoupress.com | @andyoupress

Print ISBN: 978-1-965852-56-9
Ebook ISBN: 978-1-965852-55-2

Dear Reader,

Thank you for diving head first into this steamy tropical ride with Slater and Hannah. Writing their chemistry—and watching it explode—was an absolute dream.

This story was born somewhere between a sun-drenched daydream and the many *what-if* scenarios that run through my mind on the daily.

What if two people who can't stand each other got stuck together with no cell service, no escape plan, and nowhere to go? What if the only thing they had . . . was each other? Add some ocean air, a makeshift shelter, and a spark that catches a little too quickly, and *Unexpected Destinations* was born.

Writing this short story—which was originally published in *Just One . . .: A Summer Romance Anthology* by And You Press—and expanding their journey into a novella was a joy (and a bit of a heatwave!). I hope it gives you as many butterflies as it gave me.

I've included a playlist of songs that I think capture the mood, heat, and heart of the story. Feel free to hit Play and let the story linger a little bit longer.

Thank you for reading and for trusting me to take you somewhere a little feral, a little messy, and very, very fun.

With love,

Cora

*To my husband—the one I'd follow into any
coconut grove. I love you.
—C*

Unexpected Destinations: The Playlist

"She Hates Me" – Dierks Bentley
"Cool for the Summer" – Demi Lovato
"Dancing With A Stranger" – Sam Smith & Normani
"Talk" – Khalid (feat. Disclosure)
"Cruel Summer" – Taylor Swift
"Come Through" – H.E.R. (feat. Chris Brown)
"Hawái" – Maluma
"telepatía" – Kali Uchis
"Kiss Somebody" – Morgan Evans
"Dress" – Taylor Swift
"So It Goes . . ." – Taylor Swift
"Never Be the Same" – Camila Cabello
"Good for You" – Selena Gomez
"Touch" – Little Mix
"Que Calor" – Major Lazer (feat. J Balvin & El Alfa)
"Brillo" – J Balvin (& ROSALÍA)
"positions" – Ariana Grande
"Electric" – Alina Baraz (ft. Khalid)

"Me Gusta" – Anitta (with Cardi B & Myke Towers)
"Summer" – Calvin Harris
"Thinking 'Bout You" – Dustin Lynch (feat.
Mackenzie Porter)
"Touch It" – Ariana Grande
"God is a woman" – Ariana Grande
"Body Electric" – Lana Del Rey

Chapter 1

IT'S HARD TO IMAGINE WHAT was going through my mind as I boarded that plane to Mexico, a one-way ticket in my hand and a loosely concocted plan in mind. But now that I'm here—sand caked in every crevice, saltwater nipping at my sunburned skin, alone with a couple of strangers—there's no place I'd rather be than back home, lying in bed, bingeing Netflix, snacking away my sorrows.

This vacation was supposed to be about empowerment—a chance to prove to myself that I am a strong, independent woman. That divorce doesn't equal failure. Of course, I'd pictured myself relaxing poolside for a week, a good book in hand, handsome waiters serving me cocktails—the polar opposite of how it's turning out.

But then, really, nothing in my life has turned out quite like I'd planned, has it?

Cool ocean water washes over my toes as I stand gazing out across the sea, my hot-pink polish glowing neon through grains of sand. The last time I had a view of turquoise waves like these was with Mark; Aruba's beaches were gorgeous for our five-year anniversary trip. That was before the problems between us began. Before love was no longer enough. Before the lying. Before the affair.

My teeth clench as the once beautiful memories turn sour. The image of Mark's truck in her driveway overriding every single good memory we'd ever made.

Compulsively, I pull my phone out of my small backpack and swipe open the lock screen to find SOS still looming in the top corner.

"Shit," I mutter as defeat begins to sink in.

There hasn't been a single ounce of signal since the moment I stepped foot on that boat, and apparently that's not going to change. I stare hopelessly at the useless social media apps dotted across the home screen. It seems the only dopamine rush I'm going to get right now is from imagining the look on Mark's face as he inevitably creeps on the bikini picture I posted earlier today. I'd captioned it: "Soaking up the sun in Cancun!" He'll be wondering who I'm here with. Maybe he'll post a few photos of his own to try and one-up me. But that's fine. Serves him right to be jealous. A cheater always gets what they deserve, one way or another.

What he doesn't need to know is that the joke is actually on me.

"Hey! Barbie!"

The voice snaps me out of my Mark-infested daydream.

"Dusk is setting in. Better come up here and help set up camp. Looks like we might be here a while."

I'd love to ignore the man's booming demands, but it's nearly impossible. We're the only four people here, after all.

"Coming!" I call up to him, though I doubt he can hear me over the crashing waves and the wind whipping off the ocean.

It's a short walk through the sand up to the tree line, though the trek takes more effort than expected—the dry sand swallows my feet as I trudge through the untouched beach, making each step a struggle. When I finally reach our makeshift camp, winded and clutching a stitch in my side, I'm greeted by the three people I arrived with, varying degrees of concern plastered across each of their faces.

I wrap my thin, cotton cover-up around my waist and take a seat around the fire, the dry sand pressing uncomfortably into my bare legs. The four of us eye each other awkwardly. We've had quite a few hours to size each other up after disembarking from the resort, but sitting around the fire now, the daylight fading around us, realization dawns that we might not be leaving here tonight. Suddenly, we're all new versions of ourselves—fresh and vulnerable. It's like meeting the three of them again for the first time.

"So, uh, what did you say your name was?" The middle-aged-looking man with a salt-and-pepper goatee speaks up first. He's clearly addressing the other man in the group, a thirty-something-year-old with an athletic build and an air of confidence that reeks of arrogance.

"Slater. Slater Johns. And you are?"

"Dave. Dave Edwards. And this is my wife, Julie."

Slater continues poking at the fire that he's managed to build with his "bare hands." Apparently, he's a regular Ranger Rick.

"Great to meet you both," he says, subtly raising his fire-poking stick in their direction.

A small snicker escapes my lips, and the three of them turn to stare.

"Sorry. I, um . . ."

"Problem, Hannah? Aside from the obvious one?" Slater gestures with his free hand at the miles of wide-open beach surrounding us.

I swallow hard. "'Nice to meet you' seems like a bit of a stretch, doesn't it?"

I let out a dry laugh, but apparently no one else

sees the irony, their expressions unchanged. I clear my throat, attempting to brush off the faux pas while Julie buries her face in Dave's shoulder. Slater rolls his eyes, mindlessly poking away at the flames.

"Do you think they're coming back?" Dave asks, voicing the question we're all thinking.

The abruptness of the question catches me off guard, and I brace myself for an answer, my eyes flitting around the circle, searching for clues in the others' faces.

Annoyance flickers across Slater's expression, his eyes rolling in exasperation. "Don't think like that, man. For crying out loud."

For the first time since I sat down, he turns away from the group, and I can't help but notice the clean lines that cut across his back—the kind that come from way too much time spent in the gym.

"Of course they're coming back," he continues. "They have to. They won't just leave us here. What kind of a thing is that to even say out loud?"

Dave remains silent, offering only a subtle nod in response. I watch as Julie gives his forearm a gentle squeeze.

I scoff, unable to contain myself. Who does this man think he is?

"You could be a little nicer about it, Slater. You aren't the only one stuck dealing with this mess, you know."

He turns to face me now, his brows still tightly knitted. A pang of adrenaline hits me—an all-too-familiar tension, the rush of the fight. I shake it off, tilting my head to one side, lips pursed, as he starts in.

"What's the point in talking like that? We've only just arrived here. Why start with the doom and gloom when it's not going to help anything? We've got to keep morale up. We've got to keep our heads."

The conversation ends with a stiff wave of my hand. There's no point in pushing it any further. I've known men like Slater Johns. In fact, I was married to one for seven years: alpha male, oozing with toxic confidence—probably overcompensating for his lack of emotional availability. Always something to prove. If he's anything like he's already shown—both here on the island and back on the boat—I'd say I've got him pegged: Mark 2.0.

"Since you seem to have this situation all mapped out," I start, not bothering to hide the petulance in my tone, "then I think you'll agree that it's clear we need to make a plan for tonight. We can't just sit here in a circle all night long. This wind is ridiculous. We're in swimsuits. I'm sure everyone's exhausted. So?"

I cock my head, hands folded in my lap, waiting for him to share his heroic idea.

As expected, he makes a grand show of it.

Slater shakes the sand from his long-sleeved sun shirt before slipping it over his head and shaking the fabric down over his trunk. The thin, white spandex hardly covers the sleeves of ink adorning both his arms.

I watch as his biceps tense just long enough to be noticed as he takes the fire poker into his grip. See: pure machismo. It oozes from him. He just can't help himself, not even in a situation as dire as this.

"We should definitely look for some shelter. Something to keep us out of the strong winds rolling off the ocean. It's the best way to keep warm and stay hidden. It's hard to say what predators there might be out here late at night. It'll be hot and humid offshore, but it's better than sitting out in the open. We can build a small fire to ward off any wild animals at the new campsite." He runs a hand through his dark hair, eyes fixed on me. "What do you say?"

I want to argue, to come up with something better purely out of spite. But I don't have a better idea. The ocean air is becoming too much to bear in just this bikini and thin cover-up. I can already feel the sharp sting of windburn on my lips.

"He's right," Dave speaks up. "It's what we'd do on the beaches of Hawaii during training drills. Best way to keep safe. 'Course, we were wearing full field dress and combat boots. Hotter than Hades." He looks down at his damp swim trunks and flip-flops, both covered in sand. "Nothing like this getup."

"Fellow Marine?" Slater asks, straightening his posture.

"Army. Charlie Company, First Battalion, 21st Infantry Regiment, 25th Division. Best four years of my life spent stationed at Schofield." Dave clears his throat.

"Aside from the years I've spent married to the love of my life, of course."

Julie pats his arm with a wry smile. "We're very proud of him, the boys and I."

"Ah, well, then it's settled. We should find a spot to shelter before the daylight's gone completely." With that, Slater turns and heads toward the tree line, not bothering to wait for the rest of us.

Dave extends a hand to Julie and helps her to her feet. Uneasiness grows in the pit of my stomach as I gather the few items I arrived with: my backpack, phone, and a now half-full stainless-steel tumbler. A hollow feeling of loneliness chips away at me as I realize I have no one here to rely on. The weight of this mistaken adventure rests solely on me, and whether I like it or not, there may not be a happy ending to all of this. Hesitantly, I stand and follow the group into the Mexican wilderness—alone. *If Mark could see me now.*

When I finally catch up with the others, I find Slater staring at a spot between two gargantuan trees.

"Right here should be fine," he announces, using his feet to clear away brush from the forest floor.

Panic spreads through my body like wildfire as a foul smell like rotting seafood overwhelms my nostrils. The area is buzzing with insects and choked with underbrush.

Vines tangle mercilessly around my bare ankles as I attempt to move forward, and it takes everything I have to shove the image of coiling snakes out of my mind.

"You—you aren't serious?" I ask, frantically batting cobwebs from my face.

"Yeah . . . unless you were planning on finding a Hilton Inn on this island, then by all means," Slater replies, his sarcasm palpable.

Dave and Julie exchange a quick glance before setting down their belongings and getting to work. Once again, the dread of loneliness creeps in, making it loud and clear that I'm stranded—the wilderness pressing in, silent and watchful, waiting for me to lose my grip. Sweat beads on my forehead, my breaths coming hard and fast as I stand motionless.

"You alright, Hannah?" Dave calls.

Slater turns his head, eyeing me from his area of camp.

"I'm fine," I lie, attempting to convince us all that I'm not internally panicking.

As we begin to set up camp, the sobs and sniffles coming from Julie's direction are hard to ignore, and I fight back my own tears as I lay down my cover-up on top of a pile of palm leaves—my feeble attempt at a makeshift cot. Mosquitoes as big as half dollars buzz around my arms and legs as I lower myself to the ground, leaving burning red welts in their wake. Strange chirps and trills in the distance have me on edge, the threat of wild animals at the front of mind. If there's one thing I know for certain, it's that I was not cut out for the wilderness.

Chapter 2

I FORCE MYSELF TO SLOW my breathing and turn my focus to the sky, watching as the last bit of daylight fades into a deep mulberry haze through the small gaps in the trees. I picture myself back at the resort, sitting at the poolside bar in the tight, red cocktail dress I'd stuffed into my suitcase—the same one I wore for Mark on our anniversary trip. His eyes had lit up the moment I'd stepped onto the veranda, heels clicking shamelessly on the wooden boards. I can still feel the way his hands found me, slowly tracing the outline of the dress like he was memorizing it, pausing where the fabric gave way to bare skin. His breath was hot against my ear, his voice a low rasp: *"You're going to ruin me in that dress."*

The hum of salsa music spilling through the warm

night air echoes in my memory. The burn of tequila on my tongue, the press of his chest against mine as we danced, the aroma of delicious food. My empty stomach growls at the thought of fresh guacamole, tamales, ceviche—but it's his touch I'm really craving. Back when it still meant something.

So many memories were made on that trip, moments of love and laughter I'll never forget. But some parts still linger sharply in my mind, haunting me. They stand out now like glaring warning signs—red flags I might have noticed but chose to ignore.

I can still feel the way his piercing stare settled over me that morning we sat opposite each other at the poolside café. A sweet, young waiter had just served us breakfast pastries and tea. I dug in, sampling the most beautifully displayed confections I'd ever seen, each one a work of art. A soft "mmm" escaped my lips as I closed my eyes and savored each bite. It was another morning in paradise with the love of my life—I was happy. But the way Mark's eyes darted around the room, casting glances at others around us, told me immediately something was wrong.

"Can you stop that? Geeze, Hannah, it's a damn breakfast pastry for god's sake."

I'll never forget how he stole my joy right there, like he was policing happiness. Like I was the embarrassment. One of the many times I wish I'd seen the signs.

The bittersweet memory dissolves at the sound of

loud grunts coming from Slater's side of camp. He's obviously working away at some type of elaborate shelter, although I'm not sure why—he's so convinced someone will be back for us any minute.

"Are you all right over there? You sound like you're having a coronary."

"I'm making a shelter. You could help, if you want."

"I'm perfectly fine right here."

Slater stops what he's doing and turns to me, the tips of his hair damp with sweat. "You're the only one out here without any type of shelter and it's going to be dark soon. But hey, suit yourself."

I can't help but roll my eyes as he gets back to work, leaving me to stew in the harsh reality of his words.

"You can join us in here," Julie calls out from their tiny lean-to. "It's not much, but you can't sit out there all night."

"I'll be fine. Thanks, though," I reassure her.

"The offer stands," Dave adds.

Minutes crawl as I adjust my position on the ground. I'm contemplating my next move when the sudden crash of a falling tree limb sends my stomach roiling. I jump to my feet.

"Change your mind?" Slater asks wryly, not bothering to look up from his work.

"I'll help," I say indignantly, slapping another mosquito away from my leg. "But only because these bugs are eating me alive over here."

"Right. Just start putting some palm leaves on top. Like this. Make sure to stagger them. We don't want any gaps."

My teeth clench at his delusions of authority. Where does he get off ordering me around? I weigh my options and decide to bite the bullet and follow his lead.

As I pick up the damp, gritty palm leaves, my mind wanders back to the years I spent appeasing Mark, choosing the high road rather than muddying the waters with opposition. Time after time I'd simply give in to his demands. And where did it get me?

Here: divorced in my thirties and stranded on an island in Mexico, taking orders from yet another man. Some luck.

"Almost done," Slater huffs as he stacks another stick against the tree.

I stare at the nearly finished product, struggling to envision us both inside.

"It's a pretty small shelter, isn't it?"

He wipes the sweat away from his forehead as he lowers himself to the ground and crawls inside. "You're welcome to build your own then. But as it stands, there's only one. And I'm not going anywhere."

My gaze darts between his shelter and my pathetic pile of leaves. "No, no. It's fine."

"Come on then."

I'm not sure what's worse at this point: being stuck here or being forced to share a shelter with this prick.

I could take Dave and Julie up on their offer to bunk with them for the night, but their shelter is even smaller and less impressive than Slater's, and that would be just as awkward. I let out a sigh, swallow my pride, and climb into the shelter beside Slater Johns.

"Welcome to my humble abode."

I release a puff of air through my lips. I'm not at all impressed with this man, and he must know it—his shit-eating grin is boring a hole through me as I adjust my position. If I can just make it through this night— through this terrible ordeal—and back to the resort, all of this will be sorted out. I can only imagine the lawsuit I could win from this.

"So, where are you from, Hannah? Tell me all about yourself."

I flash Slater a glare to let him know I'm not interested in small talk.

"Listen, we're stranded. There's nothing else to do, is there? Might as well talk."

"I'd rather not." I say curtly. "Why don't we just sleep? Though, I think one of us should stay awake, in case the boat comes back."

Slater stares, chewing his tongue in contemplation. I turn away, unwilling to play his games.

"Listen, is there a problem?"

"What do you mean?" My words slip out with a sigh.

"I mean, is there a specific reason you don't like me? Because you can tell me."

"I never said I didn't like you, Slater."

He scoffs. "You don't have to say it. It's written all over your face."

I press my lips into a thin line before plastering on a small, pointed smile. "I've just known plenty of men like you."

"Wow," he huffs. "And what's that supposed to mean?"

"It means, I know your type. And frankly, I'm over it. I came here, to Mexico, to get away from all that. And then I get stuck on a random island with you."

"Uh—I don't even know how to respond to that." He shakes his head, scratching the back of his neck.

"You don't have to respond. Like I said, we should rest. I'm sure we'll be picked up tomorrow."

A brief moment of silence passes before Slater just can't help himself.

"You know, I haven't done anything to make you think poorly of me. You don't even know me. How can you tell me you know my type? That's so . . . so . . ."

"So what?"

"So typical."

"Oh, so *you're* going to generalize *me* now?"

"You know what? Maybe you're right. Maybe we should just get some rest."

"I saw the way you reacted back there. On the boat. When the captain asked some of us to volunteer to get off so that he could get the boat back to shore. I saw what you did. You know, I volunteered right away. No questions asked. Why would I ask that sweet elderly couple to get off? Or that family with young children? It was obvious which four people needed to get off the boat. But still, you had to put up a fight. It just shows what kind of person you are."

"Excuse me? Were you even on that boat?"

"Of course I was, Slater! I'm here, aren't I?"

"Then you felt the engine die?"

"Duh."

"And you heard the captain tell us that there were too many passengers for the one remaining engine to make it back to shore?"

I don't bother answering this time. I just shake my head in a way that clearly says, *Obviously*.

"Then you heard when Dave started arguing with the captain about him and Julie staying aboard?"

"What? No. I—"

"Hannah, do you even speak Spanish?"

"Some," I say defensively.

Slater narrows his eyes. "If you were following the conversation, then you'd know that Dave was the one refusing to get off the boat. Claimed Julie was too afraid of the water to be left on the island. But I wasn't having it. Those elderly people and the children—of course they shouldn't have had to get off the boat."

"Then why were you shouting? No one else was shouting, Slater. You were throwing your hands in the air and making a fool of yourself."

"A fool of myself? Hannah, I told Dave that if he and

Julie didn't do the right thing on their own, I would personally escort them both off the boat. I won't stand by and watch people do the wrong thing. You volunteered. I volunteered. Why not them? The captain said he would be back as soon as he possibly could—once the other engine could be repaired. Was it completely sketchy? Hell yeah. But I couldn't see another solution at the time. I'd rather us be here, on land—on this island—than floating in the middle of the sea, *Titanic*-style."

We sit silently as I let Slater's words sink in. It's true that I wasn't very good at speaking Spanish. The language barrier was definitely an issue for me, but this was a touristy resort. Most people traveling here probably couldn't speak the language. I hadn't thought much of it. Could I have misread things? Possibly. Am I going to admit it? Not a chance.

"Do you really think the captain will come back for us?" I ask after a few moments.

"I was so sure when they first asked us to get off the boat. It seemed so . . . normal. But once we stepped foot on this island, watching the boat sail away without us was sickening. I'm honestly beginning to wonder if we made a mistake."

Slater drags his fingers thoughtfully along the sharp line of his trimmed beard.

"I think he'll come back. He seemed decent enough. I am starting to wonder if that charter was legit, though."

"What do you mean?"

"I mean, I'm wondering if it wasn't just a fisherman looking to take advantage of all the foreigners here on vacation. Just a man with a boat and a sign. I definitely don't think that was one of the resort's excursion boats."

My heart plummets as I realize he's probably right. The resort would have had a backup boat come rescue us—or even the Coast Guard. Numerous possibilities begin to flash through my mind. How could I have been so naive? My first solo trip—the very first day—and I've already made such a poor judgment call.

Slater's eyes fall, his expression echoing the chaos of emotion I feel inside. "I can't believe I bought into it. I was just so ready to go sightseeing. To get off the resort and explore. The guy only wanted a few pesos. I figured, why not?"

"We all bought into it," I reassure him.

For a moment our eyes meet, and something unspoken passes between us. The air grows heavy, charged with something I can't place, pulling at something deep in my chest. His gaze lingers a second too long, and the space between us tightens further. But there's no time to make sense of it, because just as quickly, we're interrupted by a low, rumbling noise.

"Is that the boat?" I ask, sitting up so quickly I nearly knock the palm-leaf roof off the shelter.

"I'm not sure. I'm going to go look. Stay here, just in case."

Slater cautiously ducks out of the lean-to, motioning with one outstretched hand for me to stay where I am. The sound continues steadily, growing louder and longer by the second. My heart races at the thought of the wild animals that could be lurking around our campsite.

"You guys okay?" I hear Slater whisper to Dave and Julie. "What's that noise?"

"Sorry, Slater. It's Dave. He's got sleep apnea. Needs a CPAP machine at night. He fell asleep."

Dave snorts and grunts awake, recognizing the presence of Slater standing near his shelter. "What's going on? Is the boat here?"

"No. Sorry. I was just checking on you guys."

"You were snoring so loud, you scared the poor people half to death," Julie says with the air of someone who's been married for a very long time.

When Slater returns, the look of amusement on his face tells me there's nothing to be worried about.

"Was that really just Dave?" I ask.

"Snoring to his heart's content," he confirms.

"Oh my god!"

We share a laugh as Slater climbs back inside our shelter. I do my best to make myself small, to give him ample room to exist without our bodies touching any more than necessary. But his arm grazes mine as he leans back, and no matter how much I want to pretend that it doesn't, his touch ignites something inside me. Something I haven't felt in a very long time.

# Chapter 3

"SORRY. THERE'S NOT MUCH ROOM in here."

"No, there's not." I match his apologetic smile with a wry one of my own.

"But I don't mind if you need to move over. It won't bother me."

"Ah. So I *was* right about you," I quip.

"Here we go with this again." He shakes his head. "Listen. Ask me anything. Whatever you need to know in order for me to prove you wrong."

"Prove me wrong about what exactly?"

"That I'm not like all those other men you know."

"Okay then. What do you do for a living, Slater Johns?"

"I'm a veterinarian."

Interesting. I can't hide the satisfied grin on my face. That is certainly not what I was expecting. Not even close.

"Come on," he taunts. "What did you think I was going to say?"

"Um. Well . . ."

"Out with it."

"I was banking on personal trainer. Maybe life coach? Or professional athlete." I wrinkle my nose at him playfully.

"First of all, what's wrong with any of those careers? Second of all, I do play hockey in my free time. Which is something I don't have much of. But I enjoy playing when I can."

"Hockey," I repeat, the word escaping me almost involuntarily as a scene from one of my favorite romance novels begins to play in my mind, where it lives rent-free.

"Is there something wrong with hockey, too?"

I grin. "Not at all."

As we sit huddled together in our much-too-small shelter, the conversation flows.

Slater and I ask each other twenty questions, and I'm pleasantly surprised to learn that he isn't quite as much like Mark as I'd originally thought. Slater likes books. He likes to travel. He likes sports and the gym, but not to the extent of self-obsession I originally had pegged him for. He loves animals and has a cat back home named Chester.

"I know this situation—this whole boat-ride nightmare—has just been awful. But I'm glad I met you, Hannah. You're pretty cool. Even if you did profess your hatred for me before even bothering to get to know me." He nudges me playfully with his shoulder.

"I'm sorry about that. It's just . . . I just went through a divorce. It was finalized right before this trip, actually. It's easy to see my ex-husband's faults in other men. But that's not fair."

"That must be hard." Slater's voice is genuine, almost gentle. It catches me off guard. I'd written him off as cocky and detached, but maybe there's more to him than that easy smile and those distractingly toned arms.

"It was. But I've come out of it stronger. And I'm ready to prove to myself that I can stand on my own two feet. Make my own decisions."

"Solo travel to Mexico and get yourself stranded on an island kind of decisions?" A sly smile spreads across his face.

"Well that obviously wasn't part of the plan." I drum my nails against the hard steel of my cup. "I just hope I make it back in one piece. To start the next chapter."

"You will," he says, his voice growing deep and serious. "No matter what happens with the boat, we'll figure it out. We won't give up without a fight. You'll make it back for your next chapter. Promise."

Slater extends a pinky, waiting for mine to seal the

deal. As we link our fingers together and shake on it, I feel the same surge of sparks that I felt earlier. This time, I think he might feel it, too, because he doesn't let go.

A rush of warmth burns in my cheeks. This was not supposed to happen. Not here. And not with someone like Slater Johns.

"Wait—is that Dave again, or—"

"Shh . . ." Slater holds a finger up to his lips, signaling me to keep my voice low.

We sit completely silent for a moment, listening as rustling sounds echo from behind the shelter. A low, deep growl accompanies the noise, and soon enough, it's apparent that we're dealing with something much worse than Dave's sleep problems.

"Stay perfectly still, Hannah," Slater warns. "I'm going to take a quick look."

"Slater, no! What if it's something dangerous?"

"I'm just going to take a peek—see what we've got. Just stay quiet."

I sit helpless on the jungle floor as Slater moves stealthily toward the edge of the shelter, his lower half still inside while his upper body leans out, carefully parting a pair of palm leaves.

My mind spirals with worst-case scenarios. This shelter isn't nearly strong enough to keep out a wild animal—not even a small one. It's almost unbelievable to think that we've been left to fend for ourselves, completely exposed to whatever predators might be lurking on this island. We're completely defenseless. And what about Dave and Julie? Are they asleep over there, unaware that something could be stalking them in the dark? Or worse, are they already in trouble? My heart pounds like a drum in my chest as panic sets in. I dig my nails into my thighs, desperate for a distraction.

"Hah! Get outta here! Go on now! Go!" Slater bellows, tearing out of the shelter without warning, leaving me breathless and alone as I sit cowering on the ground.

The sounds of rocks being pelted through the trees echoes in the distance, followed by more yelling from Slater.

"Hey, what's going on out here?" I hear Dave ask. "Everything alright?"

"Just an animal. It's gone now, I think," Slater responds, out of breath. "You can go back to sleep. I don't think it's coming back. I'm going to stoke the fire, just in case."

"Nice work, buddy."

A moment later, Slater's back, fresh beads of sweat glistening across his brow. "You okay?"

"Yeah, I'm fine. What was that?" I ask, scooting over.

"Coatimundi, I think."

"Um, a what?"

"A coatimundi. They're more curious than anything—

think of it like a tropical trash panda." He lets out a knowing laugh, though I have no clue what he's talking about. "Kind of like a monkey-raccoon-lemur thing. Not really dangerous unless they've got babies around. It's getting dark and they're mostly nocturnal, so it was probably just curious. Hopefully the fire and my yelling scared it off."

"If those things are out here, who knows what else is lurking around." My face must show my anxiety, because Slater's tone softens with concern.

"Hey, listen. I know that being out here is scary. Heck, I'd be lying if I said I wouldn't rather be back at the resort, lounging in the AC myself. But the way you held it together just now—that was really brave. I'm proud of you."

I bite my bottom lip and look away. "Uh . . . thanks. You were, too."

"I stoked the fire and added more kindling to keep it burning strong for a few more hours. That should keep most animals at a safe distance. And honestly, I'm not tired at all—must be the adrenaline. So I'll stay awake and keep an ear out for any noises. You'll be safe tonight. Don't worry."

My heart stumbles as I let out a breathy laugh. "Look at you, my knight in sweaty swim shorts."

"That's me."

We share a laugh, but the feeling of being protected lingers in my chest. The warmth of being cared for is almost too much to process as I let his words sink in.

"You know," Slater starts, his voice smooth and comforting. "I never would have imagined this trip could have turned out this way. Heck, this is something you see in a movie, or read in a cheesy romance novel." He breathes a laugh. "But now that it has, and we're here . . . what I'm trying to say is that I'm glad it's you I'm stuck with, Hannah."

His gaze meets mine, and for the first time, I notice how stunning his green eyes are in the flickering light of the fire.

"It could have been a lot worse," I say with a flirtatious smile. "You could have been left here with all those kids."

Slater matches my playful tone. "Yeah, or the old silver set."

"Slater!"

"Well, I'm just saying. It could have been one of them snuggled up with me in this hut."

"Is that what we're doing? Snuggling?"

"Well, I mean . . ."

Through the dim firelight, I manage to make out a hint of crimson as it rises to his cheeks.

"Only kidding," I say, lightly tapping his thigh.

His eyes travel to the spot where my fingers grazed his bare skin, just below the hem of his Americana swim trunks. "We could be. I mean, if you want."

I bite my lower lip, averting my gaze.

"I mean, we're stranded. On a gorgeous beach in Mexico." He bats his hand toward a stray palm leaf dangling overhead. "Might as well make the most of our vacation. Unless . . ."

"Unless what?"

"Well, I wouldn't want to come across too forward. Wouldn't want you thinking I'm some kind of Don Juan."

I snort a laugh. "Oh, Señor Johns. Your Spanish is muy excelente."

"Wow. We'll have to work on that." He flashes a bright smile that reveals a single crooked eyetooth.

"Will we?"

"Of course," he replies, his voice taking on a low, silky tone. "We've got plenty of time."

Slater's hand reaches up and grazes my cheek. I close my eyes briefly, leaning into his touch. I'm not sure what's happening, but whatever it is, it's too late to stop it now.

"You had sand on your face," he whispers into my ear, so close I can feel his breath tickling my neck.

I pull back sharply as every ounce of my dignity is sent packing.

"Just kidding," he breathes, closing his eyes and pulling me close once again.

The gentle pull of his hand in my hair brings me back to myself, and for a moment, everything else fades.

His lips find mine, again and again, my body drawn to him like the pull of the sea.

"Is this okay?" he asks, catching his breath. His eyes are fixed on mine as his touch glides over my shoulder.

"Yes." My voice is barely above a whisper as I welcome him in.

But this shouldn't be okay. This is definitely *not* okay. This is history repeating itself with a different version of the same man. Isn't it?

His lips trace the outline of my neck as his fingers slip beneath the thin strap of my bikini. My focus narrows to the flame building between us in this small space we share. It's a feeling I haven't experienced in so long, one I hadn't realized I'd been craving. My breath hitches as I give in to every last desire, the rumble of ocean waves in the distance the perfect soundtrack as we claim this place, making it our own.

"I could watch you fall apart for me all night." His soft lips brush against my neck as he speaks.

My eyes flutter open, a shiver rolling through me at the heat behind his words. A slow, wry smile curls across his face. He knows what he's doing to me, and it's obvious he's enjoying it.

"Slater . . . I—"

But the words catch in my throat as he dips between my legs, stealing the breath from my lungs until my thoughts disappear.

So this is Slater Johns.

Chapter 4

EARLY THE NEXT MORNING, THE sky above the island is a delicate blend of blush-flecked blue and the sun is already kissing the sea with its warm, golden rays. Slater sits beside me on the shore, watching the seagulls dive in and out of the water, his hand planted firmly in the sand.

"When do you think they'll be here?"

"Soon," he answers just a little too quickly, leaning in to kiss the top of my head.

I don't bother to act like I believe him, and I decide to change the subject. "When are you supposed to return home?"

"Actually, my flight leaves Saturday, but I wasn't planning to return home just yet. My next stop will be

Roatán, Honduras. To see the Barrier Reef. They have superb diving. Crystal-clear water."

"Sounds amazing."

"Yeah," he sighs regretfully. "Hopefully I can still make it."

"You will," I say, though I'm not sure either of us are buying it. "Were you taking some time away from work?"

"Three weeks. It's tough to get away from the clinic, especially for that long. But a break was long overdue. What about you?"

"Well, my flight home is . . . open ended."

Slater raises an eyebrow questioningly.

"I haven't booked my flight home yet. It's a bit risky doing it that way, sure. But this solo trip was kind of a last-minute decision. Maybe even a reckless one." I shift my eyes to the sand.

"I think that's really brave of you."

"You do?"

"Yeah, I mean, why not travel while you can? Do it your way. However you want to work it."

"That's what I said." Everything inside me smiles. Slater Johns and I, on the same wavelength.

"You still never told me where you're from," he says, stroking his beard in the way I've noticed he does when he's thinking something over.

"Milwaukee. What about you?"

"Rockford."

"Ah."

A silence falls between us, and I can tell we're both thinking the same thing: that's too much distance to be considered close but too close to be considered distance.

"Maybe I'll see you around sometime. I mean, after we're rescued off this island."

I shoot Slater a look, though he doesn't seem to notice. Discussing home causes a shift in mood after the excitement of last night. Anxiety begins to swell in my chest.

What am I even doing here? How well do I even know this man? Left to my own devices, I've done nothing but stumble from one mistake to the next. I need to go home—to get back to my routine, to straighten out what's left of my life.

Only, I can't. Not now and maybe not anytime soon. How long does a boat motor repair even take?

Worst-case scenarios swirl in my mind as my eyes stare, unfocused, out to sea.

"Hey," Slater gently lifts my chin, turning my face to meet his. "Everything's going to be okay. You know that, right?"

Then, with the same tenderness he showed me last night, he kisses me, holding me close as he breathes me in. He tastes salty, like a day at the beach, and once again, I find myself leaning into him, relaxing against his touch.

"Uh, excuse us . . ." A voice comes from behind, and we both startle.

"Oh, uh, good morning, Dave, Julie." Slater's voice is strained and breathy as he addresses them.

"Good mornin' there. See you two are gettin' on just fine." Dave laughs, shaking his head back and forth. Julie slaps his arm.

"I'm glad to see everyone made it through the night okay," she says. "Have you seen any sign of the captain yet?"

"Not yet. But they'll be coming for us today. Don't worry," Slater assures her, his tone transformed, back to business as usual.

How is it that this man, the same one I would have bet the bank on as being an egotistical prick just yesterday, is the one who's single-handedly keeping us all afloat here on this island? His assertiveness, his leadership, the way he reassures us all at exactly the right moments—I can imagine those qualities are part of what makes him a great doctor.

I watch as Julie's shoulders soften and Dave's worried expression relaxes.

Whether Slater actually believes we'll be going home or not, I can't be sure. But one thing I'm now certain of is that, without him, this whole thing could have gone a completely different way.

"So, what's on the agenda for the morning then?" Dave asks, though I sense he's half joking.

"I think I'll go exploring. Not far—just enough to

see what else is here. Maybe we can find some fresh water or fruit. Something useful," Slater says, getting to his feet.

"Sounds great, I'll join you," Dave chirps, wiping his hands on his swim trunks. "Might as well make myself useful."

Julie's horrified expression tells me she does not approve of Dave's adventurous offer.

"Ah come on, Jules, you'll be alright here with Hannah for a few hours, won't ya?"

"A few hours! Dave, you can't handle a hike like that through the jungle—you can't even handle a walk around the block! You won't last thirty minutes out there!"

Dave shakes his head and opens his mouth to speak, but I beat him to the punch.

"Why don't I go? You two can stay here and keep an eye out for the boat. I hike all the time at home. So it's really no trouble for me. If we find anything worthwhile, we can figure it out then."

Slater flashes a grin in my direction that I pretend I can't see.

"Fabulous!" Julie says, flooded with relief. "Thank you, sweetheart. That's a wonderful plan, isn't it, dear?"

"Yeah. Sure. Thanks, Hannah," Dave says, though I can sense his disappointment.

As Dave and Julie make themselves comfortable on the beach, Slater and I start toward camp.

"I'll just grab some water before we go," I say, realizing that I only have half of what I brought left.

"Yeah, me too. I'm hoping we can find some fresh water out here, though it's probably not likely."

I feel what little hope I was carrying fade. "Why do you say that?"

"Well, for starters, we're surrounded by the ocean and sitting at a fairly low elevation. I highly doubt there's going to be any rivers or streams flowing through here anywhere. Then you have the limestone."

I raise an eyebrow. "Limestone?"

"Well, yeah. I mean, the Yucatán Peninsula is nearby. It's known for being made up of limestone—terrible for retaining fresh rainwater. All the surrounding islands are likely to have similar geography."

My eyes widen, caught somewhere between shock and fascination. "Wow. You're just throwing surprises out left and right, Slater Johns."

He lets out a throaty laugh while using his feet to clear the brush. "Surprises?"

"I mean, who knew you were a walking encyclopedia?"

"In addition to my other talents, you mean?" He gives me a small once-over, smiling like he already knows the answer.

"Mmm, full of ourselves, aren't we?"

"Hey, you wanted to talk about me. Let's talk about you. What do you do, Hannah?"

The sound of my name on his lips sends a pulse tearing through my tangled mess of feelings as we trudge through the wilderness.

"I told you last night, it's not that interesting. I work from home, mostly. Digital marketing."

"Digital marketing. That's a great field to get into nowadays. Working from home has its perks, too, I'm sure."

Tree limbs crack and break as Slater pushes forward, clearing a path deeper into the forest. I'd love to tell him how suffocating it feels to be stuck in the house day in and day out. How it makes leaving ten times harder when the chance finally comes. How it wrecked my last relationship—how my ex decided it wasn't worth his time to be with someone so unadventurous and predictable. How he needed someone more spontaneous. More interesting. More alive. But I don't bother. Let him think my life is cool, even if he's just being polite.

"How do you know so much about the wildlife here? I mean, you seemed pretty educated about that coatimundi last night. Don't tell me you treat those at your clinic."

Slater lets out a genuine laugh—one that brings a smile to my face.

"Nah, not a lot of coatis coming in for nail trims and vaccines back home." He grins, shaking his head. "Actually, I did part of my fourth-year internship at the San Diego Zoo. There are a few coatis there. I know a little bit about a lot of animals. But I'm only an expert on a few."

"And which few would those happen to be?"

He stops and turns to face me, tree limbs shifting gently behind him. "I've found I'm very good at handling the ones who need a gentle touch." His eyes glint with a playful mischief before he turns back to the path and keeps walking.

I arch a brow, watching him go. *What in the world have I gotten myself into?*

I swat a mosquito away from my face as I eventually catch up with him. "So when will we know we've gotten to where we're going?"

Slater clears leaves with both hands, peering through brush beyond the path we've been walking. He lets out a sigh, and a grin spreads across his face.

"I think we're here. Take a look."

"What?" I ask, clambering forward. "Here, where?"

He holds out a hand and I take it, hoping he can't see the added color his touch brings to my cheeks.

"Are those . . ."

"Coconuts. It's a coconut grove." His eyes brighten, a smile tugging at his lips. "Come on."

Chapter 5

I LET SLATER LEAD ME through curling vines and brush until the dense jungle is all but behind us. What's in front of us now is a wide-open haven of towering palms. The sandy ground before us is littered with hundreds of cracked coconut shells and fallen palm fronds. For as far as I can see, the jungle has given way to a beautiful oasis.

"I guess you happened to know that coconut groves are prevalent on islands around the Yucatán Peninsula, too?" I snicker, bending to pick up a hairy, brown coconut from the ground.

"Would it impress you if I said yes?"

I shake my head, scanning the ground for something to crack the coconut with.

"Don't bother." I say, trying to hide the playfulness in my tone. "You aren't impressing me in the least."

"Is that right?"

"It is. In fact, I'm still rather *unimpressed*, Slater."

I feel his presence growing closer behind me as I stand bent forward, digging among the cracked shells and debris. Slowly, I stand, a large, smooth rock clenched tightly in my fist.

"What are you gonna do with that?" He glances from me to the rock, and I can tell he wants so badly to offer his two cents.

"I'm going to crack open this coconut. What else would I be doing?

"Want some help with that?"

I narrow my eyes. "I got it."

"By all means, baby."

My insides lurch at the casual way he throws around the pet name, like we've been using it all along. But I shake it off—there's work to be done, and I'm not going to let Slater intimidate me. I set the large, brown fruit on the ground in front of me. Drawing back with all my might, I swing. The rock makes brief contact with the shell, but when I look down, nothing's happened.

"A little advice, maybe?" Slater crouches beside a large boulder, arms raised above his head with a jagged rock in hand.

"I'm fine," I reply with a little more edge this time.

His stone strikes the green coconut with a sharp

crack. I turn to see him smiling, sniffing the broken shell before tilting it to his lips. I watch the clear, sweet liquid drip down the corners of his mouth.

"Did you want some?" He wipes his stubble with the back of his hand. "Or are you still working on that one?"

That easy grin plays on his face once again. I don't know whether it's the unbearable thirst or the traitorous flutter in my chest that betrays me first.

"Hand it over."

The warm nectar is refreshing as I gulp it down, surprised at how thirsty I am. When I lower the fruit, I'm not surprised to see Slater staring, his eyes tracing the outline of my chest.

"So are you going to share your secrets with me, or am I going to have to beg you for water every time I need a drink?"

He flashes a grin. "Well that wouldn't be so bad, would it?"

"Not what I meant."

"I'll show you. Here." He bends and picks up another coconut. "Try this one. It's green. These are the kind you want for water—easier to break open, and they've got more liquid inside. Listen."

He holds the coconut close to my ear and shakes it gently. The swishing tells me it's a good pick.

"See? This is the one you want. That brown one's too mature. It's mostly good for its meat. Much harder to crack. Alright, your turn."

His hand closes around mine as he passes me the jagged rock, guiding my fingers into place.

"Like this. Good. Now, put your coconut on a rock, not the ground. The sand is too soft."

I wait patiently as he steps behind me.

"Crouch down."

I glance back at him, hesitating.

"Go on. You don't want to be begging me for help, do you?" That same fiery grin spreads across his face.

I oblige, crouching in front of the coconut, my hands still tight around the stone.

"Now, draw back." He takes my hands in his, guiding them up over my head. "Nice and steady."

I swallow a lump in my throat as I feel him ease into me, my bikini hardly enough to buffer the press of his shorts against my bare skin.

"Now—go!" he commands, releasing my hands.

I swing, hard and fast. The shell cracks instantly, the sweet aroma of fruit filling the air around us.

"Hah!" I drop the rock and spring to my feet.

"You're a fast learner." Slater retrieves the coconut and lifts it to his lips. "That's dangerous."

He takes a long swig before passing it to me, never breaking eye contact. I reach for it, my fingers brushing his. Suddenly I feel as though all the air has been knocked out of me.

"Why's that dangerous?" I ask, fighting to keep my voice even.

He shrugs, that same smug glint twinkling in his eyes. "Because I might be able to teach you something while we're stuck here."

I bite my lip, my mouth wanting to smile so badly, but I refuse to let it. Not now. Not when I've spent the whole day pretending last night didn't happen. Not when I know exactly how his voice sounds in the dark.

I lift the coconut to my lips and take a drink, hoping the water will help cool me down. It doesn't. His gaze is still fixed on me.

"Careful," I say, handing the coconut back. "That ego might not fit in the shelter tonight."

His grin ticks up. "Challenge accepted."

He steps closer—just enough that I feel the heat rolling off his skin, sense the ease in his posture that I know is anything but harmless.

"Stop looking at me like that," I mutter.

"Like what?" His voice is low, teasing.

"Like you think you know what I want."

He leans in, lips brushing the rim of the coconut as he drinks again. "I don't think—I know."

I cross my arms like a shield against my chest, but my body betrays me. My heart races, and my skin buzzes with the memory of how his hands felt on me last night.

"You're impossible, Slater."

"That didn't seem to matter last night."

His words hit harder than I want them to, my

thoughts running in every direction. I look away, but he doesn't let the space between us stretch.

"Tell me you didn't like it. Tell me—right now— that you don't deserve to feel good, Hannah. And I'll back off."

Thick, pulsing silence stretches between us. I can't speak. He takes a slow step forward. And I don't stop him, my eyes trained on him as he closes the distance, his body pressing against mine until my back meets the rough bark of a palm tree. His eyes flick to my lips, then back to mine—like he's asking but already knows the answer. Then he kisses me—hungry and urgent, like we really are the last two people on Earth.

His hands slide down my arms, slow and deliberate, until they find my wrists. With a quiet inhale, he lifts them above my head, pressing them firmly against the tree. I'm completely pinned—the rough bark biting through the thin cotton of my cover-up and into the sensitive skin of my back, his mouth and body holding me in place.

The sweetness he showed me last night still lingers beneath his touch, but now it's laced with authority— and god, I like it. It sparks something low in my core, something that's been waiting to be undone.

"Turn around," he growls.

My breath stutters as my mind dares to form an argument. But I obey, his words hitting me with a wave of desire. I pivot slowly beneath the cage of his arms, the bark scraping against my skin and nudging me closer to his solid frame.

He releases my hands. "Keep them here," he murmurs, voice like gravel.

Slowly, his touch travels to my waist, firm and unhurried, his hands guiding my hips a fraction away from the tree. A brush of stubble ghosts along my thigh, his breath warm against my skin, until I feel the slow tug of a knot slipping loose. He lingers for a moment, as if tasting the tension—my insides squirming—before shifting to the other side. The scrape of his jaw trails a careful line across my back. Then another gentle pull as the second tie yields just as easily. The last thread of fabric slowly slips away, and suddenly, I feel the cool press of air against my bare skin, my bikini bottoms pooling at my ankles.

"Look at you." A groan escapes him as his hands trace the curves of my bare skin.

My arms fall from their place overhead, the temptation to touch him overwhelming.

"Up here," he taunts, his hands reaching back toward my wrists, anchoring them into place.

The rise and fall of my chest comes in heated succession as I wait for whatever is coming next. All at once, the warm, welcome press of his knee nudges my legs apart, widening my stance. Gentle pressure between my shoulders eases me forward until I'm fully bent at the hips. I can't hold back the gasp that rises in my throat as I realize what he's planning to do.

"You're doing so well. That's exactly where I want you," he breathes, his words thick with desire.

He drops to his knees, the subtle movement sending a ripple of awareness through me as he lingers behind me. His hands trail upward, fingers grazing my sensitive skin. Heat coils in my stomach as soft kisses map their way closer.

"Slater—" I snap upright, heart racing, unable to face him. "Slater, wait."

"Is something wrong?"

"It's just—well, I . . . we've been hiking all morning. I haven't . . . we've been stuck on this island since yesterday afternoon. I—"

I bite my bottom lip, hating myself for being so self-conscious, for ruining this near-perfect moment.

Slater leans in, his words soft and careful as he runs a hand through my hair.

"I want all of it. All of you, Hannah. Just as you are."

My pulse thunders, my thoughts splitting in every direction.

"But I—"

"Hannah, if I wanted the taste of soap, I'd try kissing a loofah."

My breath catches—a half gasp, half laugh—as his hands travel to my waist yet again.

"Can we continue?"

I nod, heart pounding, letting his steady gaze quiet the storm building in my mind. Without hesitation, he spins me with a controlled, gentle force to face the tree, positioning me exactly how he wants.

"That's it," he growls, kneeling back into place. "Let me show you how a *man* can take care of you, Hannah."

My fingers curl above my head as he moves in close, my nails digging into the bark. And then, there's nothing but the press of him, the heat of his breath against my bare skin, the slow slide of his touch—until the forest fades, and all that's left is me and Slater.

The afternoon sun casts broken shadows through the palm leaf canopies above, the dappled patterns dancing on the ground around us. Slater holds out a mature coconut, cracked and ready to eat, handing me pieces of meat he's filed off with his pocketknife.

"I've never really liked coconut. But this is actually really good," I say, still not quite sure if I'm ready to make eye contact.

"Doesn't get any fresher than this, does it?"

"Guess not." I shove another small piece into my mouth. "We should probably head back. Dave and Julie are going to start to worry."

"Yeah, maybe. Or maybe . . ." Slater lowers the coconut to the ground, reaching out a hand to touch my face.

I pull away, despite the part of me that's desperate to learn what other talents Slater might be hiding. "We really should get back. What if the boat comes and we're still out here in the middle of nowhere?"

"Feels like the middle of paradise to me." That wide smirk is back, tugging at his lips.

I shake my head, getting to my feet. "I'm serious, Slater."

"You're right. Let's grab a couple green ones for water and a few larger ones for meat, just in case we're stuck here another night."

His words sting—the thought of being stranded in the jungle another night nearly paralyzing—but I don't give them time to settle. Instead, I begin picking up and shaking a few green coconuts, setting them neatly in a pile.

"What are you doing?" he asks, eyeing me as I begin to remove my cover-up.

"Might as well make it useful." I take the garment over my head and spread it out on the jungle floor.

Carefully, I wrap four small coconuts inside and tie it closed, ready for the journey back to camp.

"Nice work," he says, his eyes catching the same light as they did earlier.

I tuck a strand of hair behind my ear, allowing a small smile to play on my face.

"You like that, don't you?"

"What do you mean?" I ask, lifting the coconuts off the ground with a quiet huff.

"I mean, that's your thing, isn't it?"

I stand frozen, the makeshift coconut sac draped over one arm, my heart pounding as I await whatever offhand remark he's about to make.

"What's my thing, Slater? Please tell me." I do my best to keep up with the act, though I can feel my walls slowly crumbling beneath his undeniable charm.

He turns his head, smiling with his teeth, before pulling his gaze back to me.

"Guess we'll just have to wait and see."

"What? Slater!"

I start after him through the palms and back into the dense jungle. There's hardly a moment to take a last look back at our beautiful oasis before it disappears through the vines and brush.

"Wait up, would you!" I call after him. "Are you going to tell me what you're talking about?"

"You mean to tell me you don't even know?"

A trickle of sweat runs down my forehead. I brush it away and raise an eyebrow at him.

"You'll figure it out by the time I'm through with you."

Slater keeps walking, his pace brisk and steady as he heads toward camp. I, on the other hand, lag behind, his words hitting me like a few extra coconuts tossed on my back. How does he manage to do this to me?

# Chapter 6

AS WE ARRIVE BACK AT the beach, the silhouettes of Dave and Julie peek through the last of the trees. When they hear us coming, each of them turn, jogging to us in unison, eager to see our treasures.

"You made it back! And what did you bring us?" Dave says, slapping a hand on Slater's shoulder.

"Let the people breathe, Dave! They've been walking all day! They're exhausted!"

Slater gives me a sideways grin. "We're definitely exhausted after that journey."

I press my lips together, letting out a quiet laugh. "It was something, all right."

"Well here, sit down. Relax. Take a load off," Dave says, ushering us to a spot in the sand near a large shade tree.

"We found a coconut grove." I toss our finds onto the sand in front of them. "Tons and tons of coconuts. Here." I pull out a green one and hand it to Dave. "Try it."

"Well, I'll be! Haven't had the pleasure of one of these bad boys since Hawaii. Wow. Talk about nostalgia."

"Slater, be a dear and help him open that, would you?" Julie says under her breath.

"I can handle a damn coconut, Julie. Come on and have a little faith in the old man."

Slater and I exchange a laugh before collapsing in the shade, coconuts in hand.

"Your turn," I say, dusting off my hands as I finish the X I've just drawn in the sand.

"Damn. You're good at this," Slater sighs, shaking his head. "Too bad you aren't as good as me."

"Excuse me?" I retort, watching miserably as he fills in the fatal space with a large letter O, ending the game.

"That's another point for me. What's that put us at now? Five to six? Five to seven?"

I narrow my eyes. "Five to five. Stick to the rules, Slater."

"Come on, I had more than five games! Who's keeping score anyway? I need to make a formal complaint!"

I can't help but laugh, an unfiltered, sun-drenched sound that bubbles out before I can stop it. Maybe it's the heat making me delirious—the hours we've spent lying here in the sand. Or maybe it's him.

He flashes a grin back, but the curve of his mouth shifts, softening into something slower, deeper. His eyes drop to my mouth, lingering there. The air between us tightens, charged with the secrets we left behind in the grove.

"So you like to play by the rules, do you?" His voice is low and smooth, and my body automatically reacts.

I clear my throat, suddenly aware of how dry my lips feel. Of how he's leaning closer. How the humid breeze carries the scent of the sea and something darker—him. Sweat and spice, coconut and sin.

His hand brushes against my bare thigh, my breath stuttering against the memory of our night in the shelter. Behind us, palm trees sway in the breeze, the ocean crashes mercilessly against the shore. But all I can focus on is the way his gaze has latched onto mine—steady and searing, like a dare.

"Well, Hannah?" he murmurs. "Do you?"

"I—" I start, my voice breathless and desperate.

"Hey! Hey, what's that?" Dave yells, a note of concern in his tone.

We all stop, halting all movement and silencing our voices as we listen to find the source of the noise. A deep hum emerges from somewhere in the distance. The sound grows louder and louder as we crane our necks.

"They're coming! They've come back for us!" Dave shouts, radiant with relief.

The words slice through the moment like a blade. Slater and I lurch to our feet.

"It's a boat!" I exclaim. "Look!"

A small vessel appears just over the horizon, speeding nearer as we all stare, using our hands to shade our eyes from the blinding sun.

"I knew they'd be back!" Julie says, slapping Dave's knee. "I said it all along!"

Slater and I exchange a glance of overwhelming joy before erupting with laughter and embracing each other tight.

"See. You're going to get your next chapter." Slater's breath tickles my ear as he holds me close.

"And you're going to Honduras."

"Well come on, you two! Let's get off this god forsaken island now, how 'bout it?" Dave's shouts break our embrace, pulling our attention back to the boat.

"Come on. Let's get out of here." Slater takes my hand as we head toward the shore, the boat idling just beyond the surf.

The minute we are safely seated on the captain's boat, my island-mates begin hurling questions, demanding to know why we were left to fend for ourselves for so long.

"But how could you just leave us like that! On a barren island with nothing! Overnight! We were terrified!

Thirsty! Starving! Shame on you!" Julie doesn't hold anything back as she allows the fear and anxiety of the previous day to erupt.

Heated conversation is exchanged in Spanish between Slater and the captain as we sail back to the resort. This time, the fervor behind his words is nothing short of admirable. The veins straining in his neck only make it harder to look away—taut, pulsing proof of what's simmering beneath the surface. I find myself nervously fidgeting with the strap of my life vest, picking at the frayed edge with my nail as I wait for what I hope will be a perfectly logical explanation.

"He says the motor was beyond repair. It took him all day to travel into town and find a new one," Slater relays to us, though he doesn't sound convinced. "Says he tried to have someone bring him out on another boat to rescue us sooner, but the wind made it too dangerous to sail. Had to wait till morning."

When I glance back at the captain, he folds his hands and raises them toward me, offering an apologetic gesture. I return it with a flat-lipped smile, although what I'd like to say to him wouldn't require translation.

Racing thoughts accompany me on the rest of the journey. How will things work out once we get back to the resort? Will Slater go one way, while I go another? Is that even what I want?

Just yesterday I was certain that Slater was exactly the same kind of man I did not want to involve myself with. But there's just something about him—something solid and grounding. He looks at me like I matter, touches me like he means it. And if I'm being honest, I like it. More than I want to admit. But what if, to him, I was just a convenient distraction? Maybe it was just the island. The sun, the novelty, the fact that we had no one else.

Soon enough, I'll have my answer. Relief fills my soul as the resort finally comes into view. Mariachi music playing over the loudspeakers floats across the water—further reassurance that we've made it. The grand, white condominiums that tower high above the sparkling, azure pools remind me that, in just a few short moments, I'll be reunited with civilization. Clearly, the paradise we left behind is alive and well, as if we'd never been gone.

The small craft pulls into a slip with a gentle thud, and the captain grabs hold of a thick, white rope anchored to the dock. One by one, we exit the boat, each of us more grateful than ever to be back on land.

"What do we do now?" I ask, directing the question mainly at Slater, though everyone seems to be contemplating the answer as we gather our bearings. "Should we go to guest services and report this? Do we call the police?"

"They'll never get away with this!" Dave grumbles, loud enough that I'm all but certain the captain must have heard. "They'll be hearing about this back home, too! News stations, social media. The whole shebang!"

"Calm down, dear. Let's be grateful the man at least came back for us. I shudder to think what would've happened if he hadn't. . . ." Julie's voice trails off.

"Listen, everyone, just keep calm. I've got the captain's name. We've all seen the boat to give a detailed description. Let's just see if the captain will come to guest services with us so we can get this ironed out. I'm sure they can help us come to a practical reconciliation." Slater gives my hand a squeeze. As per usual, he's the authoritative voice of reason that we need, and all at once, it's settled.

"Let's go then. I don't know about the rest of you, but I'm starved," Dave says, nudging Julie.

VRRRAAAMMM!

Behind us, a boat motor roars to life, a heavy spray of water coating the docks in its wake.

"What the—" I start, wiping droplets from my sunglasses.

"Hey! Get back here!" Slater bellows.

"You won't get away with this!" Dave yells, waving his fist high in the air.

But it's no use. The boat is already gone, speeding back out to sea—and so is the captain.

Chapter 7

THE FOUR OF US SIT, exchanging questioning glances as a mustached officer in an all-beige uniform jots down our names on a sheet of paper. The police station is cramped and humid, the sterile white walls stark and unwelcoming.

I focus my nervous energy on a single faded infographic hanging on the wall beside me, translated into English: *Dial 911 in case of emergency.*

Slater's hand rests on my knee, his thumb offering the occasional comforting stroke. He must sense my nerves, the way this place stirs a prickling dread inside of me. The way that just being here has slowly unlocked traumatic memories with Mark that I can't seem to shake. But I welcome Slater's calm, his grounding presence that somehow softens the sharp edge of it all.

"This sort of thing happens from time to time," the policía explains, snapping my thoughts back into focus. "As hard as these resorts try to keep unauthorized people from selling their services to vacationers, it's nearly impossible to enforce. Without proper permissions, your average person shouldn't be able to trespass on resort property and claim they're offering boat-ride excursions to remote places. But the ocean is tricky territory. Technically the resort can't kick those people out of the water. The only thing we can do is warn tourists to stay on the resort, or utilize resort-guided excursions only. Many people see through the scams, but occasionally—"

"Now wait just a minute," Dave starts, a rigid scowl plastered on his face. "You're sayin' it happens from time to time that people like us get left on deserted islands? You're blaming us for this mess?" He points a finger in the officer's direction, which Julie promptly swats away.

"No, sir. What I'm saying is that, unfortunately, you all boarded an unauthorized vessel, and with that came a terrible consequence. It is only fortunate that the man returned for you. Those small boats are not made for such long journeys across the ocean. It is no surprise he had to turn back. Ten passengers? Way too much weight for two small engines on a ship that size."

"How were we supposed to know that?" I ask, my eyes darting desperately between the officer and Slater.

"He had a very professional sign and everything," Slater adds. "It even had the resort logo on it, if I'm not mistaken."

"You're absolutely right, Slater," Julie interjects.

"I can promise you that we will be on the lookout for this boat. If we find it, we will be sure to investigate the situation."

"If?" Slater clenches his jaw. "These criminals need to be held accountable, sir. There's no *if* about it."

"There are thousands of boats in Cancun alone, Señor. Most of them are unregistered and unregulated. We will do our best. Of course, the resort has been notified, as well as surrounding resorts, and we will do our best to alert new travelers to participate in only resort-certified excursions." The officer folds his hands on top of his desk. "Please, if there's anything else we can assist you with, you let us know."

"Slater . . ." My voice cracks.

"I know," he says calmly. "I know."

Chapter 8

DESPITE MY DISAPPOINTMENT AT REALIZING the man responsible for scamming us into a night alone in the wilderness would likely never be held responsible, the rest of the week at the resort was filled with dancing, great food, and most surprisingly, Slater.

"These have got to be the best tamales I've ever eaten."

I take another bite, savoring the rich flavor. Good food hits differently after being deprived of it for so long, even if we have been back at the resort for a few days.

Slater snickers, grinning as he takes a slow sip of his drink, watching me over the rim of his glass.

A flicker of anxiety twists in my stomach. I lower my fork and dab at my lips with my napkin. "What?"

"You," he says, still smiling.

"Oh. Um . . . sorry." I glance down, placing the napkin back in my lap.

"Sorry?" He laughs softly. "God, no. I was just thinking, you're so damn cute when you're happy."

My eyes flick back to his, uncertain. "What?"

"The way you look when you're enjoying yourself." His tone shifts, softer now. "You're beautiful, Hannah. I couldn't look away if I tried."

I blink, completely caught off guard, unsure how to respond. No one has ever looked at me like Slater is looking at me right now—like I'm something worth admiring for just being me. Mark would have rolled his eyes. He would have told me to tone it down and made sure I wasn't embarrassing him. But Slater? This is all new territory. It shouldn't feel so foreign to be complimented, to be valued and loved by someone like this, but it does. And god help me—that might be why I'm falling for him faster than I know I should be.

Slater doesn't look the least bit uncomfortable as I shift awkwardly in my seat. I scramble for something—anything—to say, but the words stick in my throat.

"Tomorrow is Saturday," I blurt out at last, grasping for anything to steer the conversation back to solid ground.

Again Slater looks at me over the rim of his margarita. "It is."

"All packed for Honduras?"

"Just about. Still a few things left." His voice dips, and immediately I feel bad for bringing up the end of such a great week.

"Just don't go riding any sketchy boats across the ocean out there, okay?" My tone is playful, though the thought of him leaving is suddenly overwhelming.

"Why, you don't think I can survive on a deserted island twice?" A wide grin plays on his face.

"I have no doubt that you could. But I think I might miss getting to talk to you."

His smile widens. "Me? Are you sure? Because I thought you hated me?"

"Give it a rest." I scoff.

"I'll miss you, too, Hannah."

We go back to sipping our cocktails, neither of us completely sure what we want to say next. One week ago, I was a divorcee, stepping off a plane alone in another country to prove that I could do hard and adventurous things all by myself. To prove that I didn't need Mark to dictate my life any longer. How have things changed so much in only seven days? Sitting here now, across from a man who was a total stranger not long ago, I watch the gleam in his green eyes—reflecting an understanding of a shared experience only we can fully grasp—and I realize: everything has changed.

Today, my heart aches for a whole different reason. But it doesn't make sense.

No one falls for a perfect stranger on vacation.

Do they?

My phone pings in my purse beside me, barely audible over the music.

"Sorry. Let me just—" I dig through the small crossbody, stealing a quick glance at the screen before switching the notifications to silent.

Finally, a text from Maya. The temptation to read what she's sent is agonizing. But I refuse to be that person—pulling out my phone to have a side conversation at dinner. I look up to find Slater flashing a smile that reveals his crooked eyetooth, and the hand holding my phone instantly sinks below the table.

"I'm sorry. It's my best friend, Maya. She's been texting me nonstop after I told her about our little excursion to the island. She's just being a good friend. Checking in. A lot." I huff out a quiet laugh, shaking my head.

"Oh, so, you told Maya about *our* excursion then?"

"Not all of it. Just the gist of it. The part about getting stranded and then miraculously saved again the next day. You know, the important stuff."

"Ouch." He inhales sharply through his teeth, swirling the straw in his water glass.

"Only kidding." I place a hand on his, the soft clink of my bracelets catching the lights above us. "I might have mentioned meeting someone."

He raises an eyebrow, a smile creeping across his lips. "Oh, did you? And what did you tell her?"

"Just that he's the biggest tool bag I've ever met."

"Okay, now you're in for it," he says, his voice playful, but that look of desire is already creeping back into his eyes.

I drop my gaze to my plate, trying to steady myself.

"But seriously. That's why she's blowing up my phone. She just wants to make sure I'm okay. That I'm safe with whoever I'm with. I need to call her."

"It's great that you have a close friend who cares about you like that."

"She's been a godsend during the—over the last few months. I don't know how I would have made it through without her."

Silence falls over the table, the near mention of the divorce looming between us like a storm cloud waiting to break.

"So," Slater says, breaking the silence, "have you figured out your plans? Do you think you'll stay here a little longer?"

"Uh, yeah. Maybe. I'm not actually sure."

"Well you deserve it. Relax, read your books. I feel bad I distracted you so much this week. You hardly got to enjoy them."

"Don't feel bad," I say, blushing. "I may stay a few more days. Dave and Julie are here an extra week."

"I heard the resort comped their stay and gave them a free week for their troubles," Slater says, scooping guacamole onto a tortilla chip.

"Can't say I blame them."

"Yeah, I guess not. It's just, it didn't turn out half bad for me after all."

I smile, tucking a strand of hair behind my ear. "I could say the same."

Slater grins, straightening in his seat.

"Another drink, Señorita?" A waitress dressed in a brightly colored floral-patterned blouse holds a tray next to the table.

"No, thank you," I say, covering the top of my glass with my hand.

Slater declines as well, and eventually we make our way outside, following the pulsing rhythm of tamboras and maracas. I stop to kick off my wedges, the feeling of the sand between my toes freeing as we walk. Slater's hand brushes the back of mine before we gently lace fingers, the feeling instantly transporting me to our time spent huddled under the palm leaves.

"You should text your friend. She's probably worried about you. I can wait."

"Are you sure? I can do it later. She's probably putting her kids to bed or something anyway."

"Really, I don't mind. It's important. I'm not going anywhere." He throws me a wink, rendering me all but useless.

"Okay. It won't take long."

"I'll get us some drinks," he says, stepping past me. As he does, his hand lightly brushes against the small of my back—just enough to send a flicker of heat through me.

I stay still for a beat longer than I should, watching him disappear into the crowd, before I finally pull out my phone and head toward the edge of the dock to text Maya. When I open my messages, I find several from her—each sent within the last hour, their frantic, scattered words practically leaping off the screen.

> **Maya: CALL ME!**
> **Maya: CALL ME NOW!**
> **Maya: Seriously Hannah! Where are you! It's Mark! Call me!**
> **Maya: I don't know how much longer I can keep him from coming Hannah**

Adrenaline shoots through my veins. What is she talking about? Keep Mark from coming . . . here?

The line is slow to connect, but once I finally hear her voice, the urgency in her tone is apparent.

"Hannah! Didn't you get my messages?"

"I'm sorry, Maya. I did. I was at dinner. What's going on?"

"It's Mark. He's gone ballistic, Hannah. He showed up here, drunk. Thank god everyone was already in bed. He demanded I tell him where you were. Said he was coming to get you. That the two of you needed to talk things over. But I don't know, Hannah—"

"I'm so sorry, Maya. So, so sorry. I can't believe he would—"

"Don't you dare apologize! You are so much better than that piece of shit."

"Where is he now? Did he leave?"

"He left. Travis called the cops—though not before giving Mark a piece of his mind. They're both lucky I was here to calm Travis down."

"Oh Maya. I can't believe this. I'm so sorry."

"None of this is your fault, Hannah. You hear me? I just want you to be safe and happy. I want you free of that idiot once and for all."

"Does he know where I am?"

"Well, he knows you're in Mexico. He busted past me into the house and found the resort brochure on the counter. But I don't think he's crazy enough to actually come down there. Do you?"

A ringing in my ears keeps me from answering. Play-by-plays of past arguments start rolling through my mind—painful and unrelenting. Would Mark come all the way to Mexico to convince me of whatever delusions he has playing in his head? Suddenly the food in my stomach turns sour. I sit, my feet dangling toward the water, eyes closed as I take deep breaths of ocean air.

"Hannah? Are you okay?"

"I'm fine."

"Listen, he's locked up for the night. There's no way he's getting out, at least not until morning. So we have time to figure this out. And I promise you, I'll take care of this. If he even steps foot near an airport, alarms will sound."

A quiet laugh slips out as silent tears stream down my cheeks.

"I'm so sorry to ruin your night. You should be having fun! And you still can. There's nothing urgent happening here now. We're safe, you're safe. There's plenty of drinks to be had in Cancun. And seriously—when are you going to tell me about this *man*?"

"Oh Maya. My life is a mess, isn't it?"

"A mess? Hannah, you just spent a week in paradise with a man you just met and, knowing you, he must be something pretty special for you to let your guard down. Come on. Spill it already!"

The next fifteen minutes pass like clockwork as I try to explain the enigma that is Slater Johns to my best friend. I don't hold back—we're way past filtering things at this stage of our sisterhood.

"Lord help me," she says, all faux-dramatic. "Where can I find one of these jungle veterinarians?"

"Maya!"

"Joking, joking. Obviously. I'm happily married, Hannah."

We both laugh, the tears welling in my eyes—a mess of relief, sadness, excitement, and fear all tangled together.

"Alright listen. I promise I'll let you know if there's

anything happening here you should know about. But please, please promise me you'll do your best to forget about Mark tonight. Enjoy every single second of Slater Johns. You deserve it. Love ya. Call me if you need anything."

We end the call, my heart both full and shattered at the same time. I sit still for a moment in an attempt to compose myself, wiping at stray tears, swiping my finger in a line beneath my mascara.

When an unexpected touch brushes my shoulder, I flinch. I turn sharply to find Slater standing behind me, two brightly colored drinks in hand.

Chapter 9

"SORRY. DIDN'T MEAN TO SCARE you." Slater sets the drinks on the dock, looking out across the dark water. "Can I sit?"

"Yeah, of course," I say, attempting to camouflage the emotion in my voice.

"Everything alright back home?"

I suck in an unsteady breath. "Yeah, everything's fine—or at least, I think so. Maya was ecstatic to hear I'd met someone. She wouldn't shut up about it." I laugh, stealing a quick glance at him.

"But you did mention the part where I'm an egotistical womanizer with questionable morals and spotty integrity?" He winks, nudging his shoulder into mine. "Because that definitely would've turned her off."

"Oh, I mentioned it. She must be more desperate than ever for me to meet someone—didn't faze her in the least."

Slater and I lock eyes, the fiery rapport burning between us.

I let my gaze fall to the water, where the reflections of the tiki lights and neon signs illuminate the sea life below, turning the seaweed into sparkling shades of pink and blue.

"If there's anything else bugging you, Hannah, you know you can talk to me. Even if it's . . . you know, about something you think I might find uncomfortable. Like your ex, or whatever. I care about you. And if you need to vent, I'm here. We went through something together—something most people couldn't even imagine. Like it or not, we'll always be linked by what happened on that island. You and me. That bond? It doesn't break. I just want you to know that."

I have to look away, the soft sting of his words sending up a fresh surge of emotion that threatens to spill down my cheeks.

"Hey," he says, gently tucking a strand of hair behind my ear. "What's going on?"

I inhale a deep, settling breath. "It's my ex."

Slater gives a subtle nod, wrapping an arm around me and pulling me in close as I recount the phone conversation with Maya. I watch his expression stiffen as I mention Mark threatening to come here to talk things over. I tread carefully, avoiding any hint of our speckled past. I don't intend to drag that up tonight.

When I'm finished, it feels like a weight has been lifted, grounding me in the present.

"One thing I know, Hannah, is that no matter what, you're safe here with me. No one is going to hurt you while I'm around. I promise you that."

The certainty in his tone is palpable as he holds me, our feet dangling together over the sea. I lean into his every word, letting his safety wrap around me like the same protective net I felt back on the island.

Only, he's leaving tomorrow. And then I'll be on my own. Truly alone. Goosebumps travel in a line up my arms.

"Slater, let's just enjoy tonight."

"Okay. Anything. What would you like to do?"

"I want our last night to be the best one yet. I want to get my mind off of this whole nightmare. I want to enjoy every last second here."

There's something behind the glint in Slater's eyes that I can't quite read, something I don't recognize on his suntanned face. He leans in, one hand finding my cheek, and kisses me, the night air brushing over my damp eyelashes.

"Every last second," he whispers. "Come on."

"Where are we going?" My voice is hesitant, and my eyes search his.

"To stop thinking and start feeling."

My heart pounds louder than the music spilling out

onto the beach as he leads me out into the crowd of happy couples. The sand is alive with vibrations—speakers sending thick, heavy bass crashing through the night air. Bodies sway in every direction—dancing, laughing, glowing under the neon lights. Slater pulls me into the center, his arms wrapping tightly around me, his body moving with the rhythm, taking me over entirely.

His hands find my hips, gliding down my body as if they belong there—like he's touched me a thousand times before. I slide my arms around his neck, my fingers brushing the base of his throat. We don't say a word; there's no need. Our bodies move together, speaking a language all their own as the music guides us.

My head buzzes with heat and hesitation as the tension builds between us, and I know he's feeling it, too—that hungry, unguarded glare in his eyes returning, sharper now, like he's seconds from losing control.

Slater stops dancing, his body goes rigid, his hand finds mine.

"Come on," he mouths, though I can't hear him over the noise.

He leads me away until the sound of the thumping beat fades and we can finally hear each other again. Over my shoulder, I can still see the flicker of firelight, bodies pulsating to the rhythm, the chaos of the dance floor just barely in view.

"Where are we going?" I'm nearly out of breath, the night air thick and heavy with salt and heat.

"To enjoy every last second." His mouth curls into a smile that sends my insides rolling.

Sprays of sand kick up around my too-tall sandals as we leave the main path and slip onto the beach. I follow as Slater ducks between a couple of tall hedges and behind the stuccoed spa building I'd only glimpsed earlier in the week.

"What are we doing here, Slater?"

But my question is met again with that sly smile, and I already know I have no choice but to follow him.

The spa is silent at night—dark and mysterious. The lines and hustle from the daytime crowds have disappeared, the energy shifted to the nightlife we've just left behind. Slater pauses at a gate with a small wooden sign: *Hydrotherapy Garden 8 a.m.–8 p.m.*

"Slater, it's closed. It's like, eleven."

He flashes me a crooked, knowing smile and gently pushes on the gate. Slowly, it creaks open.

"Are we allowed in here?"

"After you." He extends his arm, pointing me inside.

"What are we doing here, Slater?" I demand more firmly this time.

"We're doing exactly what you asked. I'm making sure you have the best damn trip of your life, baby."

I hesitate for half a breath, then step inside.

Lanterns flicker low in the trees, casting golden light over stone walkways and deep, steaming pools. The loud music of the party outside fades away, replaced by the soft trickle of a water fountain and the whisper of a breeze through hanging vines. The air smells like jasmine and lavender, sacred and mesmerizing.

Slater takes my hand, leading me along the path until we reach a quiet, curved alcove where a small pool shimmers beneath a canopy of palm fronds and stars. Steam rises in thick, white curls from its surface. I turn to face him.

His eyes find mine in the low light—hungry and desperate. His hand rises to cup the side of my neck, his thumb brushing just under my jaw.

"We shouldn't be here," I whisper, my voice barely above a whisper.

His eyes drop to my lips. "That's the best part, isn't it?"

A spark races down my spine, anticipation curling like smoke beneath my skin.

"Everyone had their eyes on you back there, you know that? Can't say I blame them—you're the most gorgeous woman on this beach, Hannah." His voice is low and intoxicating as he trails kisses down my neck. "The way you move . . . you drive me crazy."

My breath shudders out as his words wrap around me, sinking deep into my core, stirring something hungry and helpless inside. My world narrows to his mouth, his hands, his touch, the sound of the water, rushed breath, and want. I reach my hands into his shirt, feeling the heat of his skin beneath the fabric, the quick beat of his heart as he explores my curves.

His fingers reach for the zipper at the small of my back—slow and deliberate. Time stands still as my body aches for his touch, his hand grazing the newly bare skin while he inches the zipper down. With the slightest nudge, the dress slips from my shoulders, gathering at my feet in a wash of red.

He pulls back a few steps, leaving me aching for him to come closer. Suddenly, I feel vulnerable, exposed without the cover of his body against mine. I look away, unable to hold his gaze, afraid he'll see just how much I want him . . . how much I don't want this to be the last time.

"Look at me, Hannah."

I oblige, a rush of uncertainty blooming like heat beneath my skin.

He exhales, low and slow. "God, you're fucking perfect." His eyes rake over my naked form, as if my very presence has sucked all the air from his lungs.

A slow-burning heat spreads across my chest, crawling its way to my face.

"Come here." He growls, eyes dark and steady, the evidence of his need for me visible through his shorts.

I move toward him, my heart pounding louder with every step. Then, his hands are around my waist, lifting me effortlessly off the ground. My legs wrap around him instinctively as he carries me toward the edge of the pool, walking us down the gentle incline until warm water rushes up to nip my bare skin. Together we glide deeper into the water, his hands locking tight around my ass.

The cool tile meets my skin, pressing against my back—grounding me for one breathless second before he fills the space between us.

"Hands up," he whispers, lips brushing against my damp skin as he guides my hands to the ledge above my head.

I grasp the ledge, my toes curling as I anticipate what's coming next.

"That's it," he breathes, rocking hard and thick into my core.

"Slater," I whimper, urgency buzzing at my fingertips.

"Every second, baby."

His hands disappear beneath the water's surface, gripping his waistband. With a practiced ease, he slides them down over his hips, water rippling around him as he steps free. A soft moan escapes my lips, unraveling him as his mouth drags down my neck, teeth grazing my nipples. I arch my back, my body desperate for more of him—*all* of him.

"You look so damn pretty with your hands above your head, Isla."

My eyes flick open, questioning.

He leans closer, voice husky. "My island girl. I've been thinking about doing this to you all day. I'm going to take good care of you now."

My body writhes beneath the weight of him and his

words as he fills me up, my back hitting the smooth tile with each thrust of his hips, water splashing around us. Rippling pleasure surges through me, the slow, steady rhythm of his movements nudging me dangerously close to release.

"Not yet, Isla," he breathes. "We have all night."

With one final roll of his hips, he thrusts out of me, leaving me panting—pulsing for him in his absence.

"Do you trust me?" he asks, his tone soft, but his eyes burning with desire.

I wrap my arms around his neck, my fingers threading into his hair, tracing the outline of his jaw. In one smooth motion, he lifts me from the water, cradling me as we exit the pool. The placement of his hands is both intentional and agonizing as we enter through a large set of billowing white curtains, soft lantern light illuminating a luxurious cabana. Droplets slip from our damp skin, soaking the silken sheets.

"On your knees," he orders, his voice thick with gravel as his hands grip my waist.

The only thing I'm sure of is that I need Slater—all of him—right now.

"You're so wet for me, Isla." His fingers glide along my pulsing center, his hard length pressing, teasing, against the back of my thighs.

"I need you, Slater. Now," I beg, my voice breathy and urgent.

A deep, primal sound escapes him, raw and unguarded. One hand grips my shoulder, fingers curling toward my neck as he thrusts himself inside me.

"You take me so well, baby." He tightens his grip, his breath hot against my skin, each thrust harder, heavier than the last. "Come for me. Now."

I can't stop the moan of pure ecstasy that bursts free as his hand finds my clit, small circling motions pushing me over the edge, completely at his mercy.

"I've got you, baby." He wraps an arm around my middle, supporting me as I tremble.

The air hums with heavy breaths, charged silence settling between us. And then I'm certain. Completely certain that Slater Johns not only knows but has mastered *my thing*.

"Good girl, Isla."

His hips slam into me one final time, his thighs slapping hard against my ass, fingers pressing deep into my skin, as he finishes in a wave of bliss. Together we collapse on the damp sheets.

"Every last minute," I whisper.

# Chapter 10

SOMEWHERE OVER THE LOUDSPEAKERS, THE bartender announces last call, signaling to the crowd to make their way to the bar or back to their rooms, leaving the dance floor emptier than it's been all night. Slater's knees press against mine as we sit facing each other atop high-backed rattan barstools.

"Want another?"

I watch him down the last of his margarita, a speck of salt clinging to his lip.

"I think I'm calling it quits." I breathe a laugh, reaching up to swipe the salt away.

"Mmm Hannah, Hannah. What am I going to do without you tomorrow?" His tongue flicks over the spot where my finger just touched.

"I dunno," I sigh, unable to come up with anything better.

He smells like lavender haze and tequila, and my thoughts race with the realization that our time here is truly coming to an end. Our last night has flown by—despite making every second count, it's still going to end.

"Come on," he says, placing a few pesos on the bar counter. "Let's get out of here."

I nod, my feet heavy beneath me. The last drink I'll have with Slater Johns. What will they think when I come here tomorrow night alone? Maybe I'll stay in, order room service. Maybe I'll have bigger things to worry about by then. I pull out my phone—no messages. Would Mark really try to come to Mexico? Will Maya really be able to stop him?

"Hey," Slater interrupts my thoughts. "Everything's going to be okay."

"I know."

"Listen, I just want you to know that this week has been one of the best I've ever had. Sure, it didn't go anything like I planned." He laughs—a nervous, awkward laugh that puts me on edge. "But I think if I had to do it over again, I wouldn't change a thing."

I swallow a lump in my throat. "I wouldn't change it either."

Slater reaches a hand around his head, scratching the back of his neck, searching for the words.

"Hannah, if I don't see you again—"

"Don't say that," I interrupt, breaking his gaze. I stare down at my toes where my slightly chipped pink polish peeks out from the sand. An entire current sweeps through the pit of my stomach.

"No, seriously. I need you to know that no matter what happens, I'll never forget you."

"I'll never forget you either, Slater."

"But if our paths don't cross again . . ."

I don't need to hear any more. I know where he's going with this. *We can still be friends, Hannah. Hit me up on the socials, Hannah.* It's nothing I haven't heard a million times before.

"I understand, Slater," I tell him, my voice sounding harsher than I intend.

"What?" His face falls, confusion clouding his features.

"You don't need to say it. I got it. We had a great week and now it's over. I understand. It was really nice meeting you. Thanks again for saving my butt out there. Oh, and for the nickname. I hope you have a really awesome time in Honduras."

I do my best to paint an expression of cool indifference on my face, hoping he can't see the tears welling in my eyes. This is stupid. What did I expect would happen? We're two different people, from two totally different backgrounds. Life can't just stop after a week of vacation gone wrong—or should I say, gone undeniably right.

I should have listened to what my gut instinct was trying to tell me all along.

Slater Johns is exactly the type of man I knew he was. I just didn't want to see it—not after that night on the island, after our week in paradise.

"Yeah, okay. Well I should probably get back to my room. I have some more packing to do before I leave. My flight is at five tomorrow morning."

I nod, fearing that just one more word will push me to the edge of a tearful breakdown. Together we walk back to the lobby, the bright fluorescent lighting no doubt giving away more of the emotion on my face than I'd like. The sudden ding of the elevator call button marks the beginning of an awkward silence that settles between us.

"I'll call you. If that's okay?" Slater says, breaking the tension.

"I'd like that."

He nods, something unspoken hanging just beneath his breath. Suddenly it's all over—the buzz of the drinks, the high of his touch, everything. All that remains is me, and a raw, aching vulnerability spreading through my chest.

"Enjoy the reefs," I manage to say just as the elevator doors slide open. I turn to leave, welcoming the escape as a tear falls down my cheek. But before I can cross the threshold, he catches my arm, his touch firm and deliberate as he pulls me back. His embrace fills me with a longing like I've never felt. This is really it. This is what it feels like to say goodbye to someone you've just met. Someone you've fallen hopelessly in love with.

"Come with me," he whispers into my ear. "Come to Honduras."

"Slater, I-I can't. We've only known each other for a week. My divorce has just been finalized. I have god only knows what going on back home. I can't drag you into my mess. I'm supposed to be—"

"So what?" he interjects. "So what about any of that? I know it's fast, but you said it yourself, you haven't even purchased your ticket home yet. Your plans can still change. You could leave this resort and come to the reefs with me. We could have one more week."

His emerald eyes are pleading with me to say yes, and it crushes me to have to turn him down—to break my own heart.

"You know, sometimes it's the unexpected destinations that end up taking you exactly where you're meant to be, Hannah."

"Slater, I can't. I'm sorry. I wish more than anything we had met at another time, or under different circumstances. But I have to—"

"Hey." He holds his hands out in defeat. "I get it. You don't need to explain yourself." He pauses, holding my gaze. "It's been a pleasure, Hannah."

For the final time, he leans in and places a gentle kiss on my cheek, the gesture seeming both sweet and irritatingly juvenile after the careful attention he's shown me this week.

"Goodbye, Slater."

Chapter 11

THE WHEEL ON MY DISCOUNT luggage vibrates as I drag the suitcase through the bustling airport. Signs point me toward customs and security, and a feeling of satisfaction settles over me as I navigate my way through: a single woman, confidently navigating the world, just as I had set out to do.

"Buenos días, Señorita." A tall, handsome man at the counter greets me pleasantly as he reaches a hand out for my passport.

"Buenos dias," I respond back, handing it over with the confidence of someone who does this sort of thing all the time.

When I finally step out into the bright sunshine, a cherry-red shuttle bus is waiting to take me to my destination. I watch as eager groups of tourists scour the lot for their rides, itinerary and phones in hand. My own phone buzzes in my pocket, and I'm instantly reminded that Maya is anxiously awaiting my arrival text.

Maya: Well?
Maya: Did you make it?

My response comes with a genuine smile—the kind that comes from knowing I have a true soul sister on my side. One who won't rest until she's sure I am safe.

Me: Just landed. About to board the shuttle bus. Won't be long now . . .
Maya: AHHH! Promise me you'll tell me all about it.
Me: Duh.
Maya: Be safe out there. No boat rides.
Me: Don't have to tell me twice.
Me: Thank you for everything. Love you!
Maya: <3 always

It's not lost on me that this trip might not have happened if it weren't for Maya—my tenacious best friend who refused to rest until my ex was completely out of the picture. And by "out," I mean arrested and charged with assault and trespassing after his little stunt the other night. Turns out, unbeknownst to either of us, he was already on the hook for a DUI. It doesn't sound like he's getting out anytime soon. And when he does, something tells me they'll be keeping a close eye on him

Up ahead, the bus doors swing open on creaky hinges and the engine hums idly as passengers begin to board. The driver steps forward, reaching out to greet me as I approach. He begins loading my bags into a stowaway compartment and motions for me to board. Excitement prickles across my skin as I climb the stairs, clutching the strap of my backpack slung around my shoulder. I choose a seat by the window in a row by myself and sit. An upbeat tune plays from staticky speakers overhead as I pull out my phone and open the last message I received from Slater.

Isla—
Don't let one bad egg ruin it for the rest of us.
Luna Del Mar Resort
West Bay Inlet, Km 4
Sandy Bay, Roatán, Islas de la Bahía
Honduras, C.A.
Just in case you change your mind.
—S

I tuck my phone back into my pocket as the driver climbs inside and closes the doors.

"Vámonos!" He gives a thumbs-up and the bus lurches forward.

As we get closer to the resort, the beauty of the island becomes apparent. The water is clearer than I could have imagined, a vibrant teal like something off the cover of a vacationer's magazine. Palm trees thrive at every turn, their green leaves striking against the blue sky.

When the bus comes to a stop, the doors open to a perfectly orchestrated row of villas, each one overlooking the ocean, their own private docks stretching out like tiny peninsulas into the sea.

"Wow," I can't help but say under my breath.

The driver ushers us into a small, stuccoed building labeled *Recepción*. I take a seat on a cushioned chair, parking my suitcases beside me. My knees bounce up and down, nervous tension searching desperately for an escape.

"Can I help you, miss?" the clerk asks in a thick accent.

"Yes. I'm meeting someone. His name is Slater Johns." It comes out sounding more like a question, but she seems to know right away who I'm looking for.

"Ah, Mr. Johns. One moment." The clerk picks up the phone, dials quickly, then waits, looking up at me occasionally over the mouthpiece.

Apprehension knots in my stomach. Was this the right move? What will Slater think of me just showing up like this? On one hand, he did invite me. But on the other, I did decline. What if he's already met someone new—someone with way less baggage? It only took us a week to fall for each other, after all.

Time feels like it's ticking backward as I nearly talk myself out of confronting him. I can't believe I'm here, chasing down this wild idea—this reckless hope—that Slater might actually be the one. Every time I let that thought creep in, it sounds more and more absurd: following a near-stranger halfway around the world in the name of whirlwind insta-love. But before I can change my mind, a familiar voice stops my thoughts right in their tracks.

"You came."

When I look up, I see Slater is standing in the doorway, sandy legs and board shorts, a look of astonishment on his face.

"I did." My own voice sounds foreign and shaky in my ears as I stand, taking a small step toward him. "I was sitting at the bar back in Cancun—alone—and someone's wise words kept replaying in my mind. Something about those *unexpected destinations*."

There's no more time for talking as he rushes over and wraps me in his sunblock-smeared arms. It's like we're picking up right where we left off, standing outside that elevator in Mexico. Right where we began on that deserted island.

It's hard to imagine what was going through my mind as I boarded the plane to Mexico, or why I thought a solo boat excursion in Cancun was a sound and sane idea. But I'll never forget that island, that co-conut grove. And I'll always be grateful for the time I spent there, for the love I found there.

"Come on," Slater says, throwing an arm around me. "We have a lot of catching up to do."

I follow him out of the lobby and into the warm sunshine of Roatán.

"You know," he starts, "I've been thinking. Rockford really isn't that far from Milwaukee."

I move my sunglasses down my nose and look at him skeptically.

"Well, I've always liked Milwaukee. Beer, cheese, Harleys. What's not to like?" He nudges me with his elbow, and I can't contain my laughter.

"Seriously? Cheese?"

"And then of course, there's my island girl."

I'm not ashamed to say I was wrong about Slater Johns as we walk hand in hand across the second island we'll conquer together.

Epilogue

A WARM, FUZZY BODY WINDS around my legs as I step into the apartment, nearly tripping me. I stumble over the mat, hands full of takeout and the last of my bags from Milwaukee.

"Really, Chester? Come on, dude. I'll feed you in a sec. You know we'd never forget about you."

Despite my reassurances, desperate meowing follows me as I deposit our dinner on the kitchen counter, breathlessly kick off my heels, and bend down to stroke Chester's back.

"Daddy will be home any minute now. You just be a patient kitty," I say, scratching his chin. "Mama's gotta get ready."

As I move to stand, Chester stares at me skeptically,

apparently starved for both attention and dinner. I'm grateful when he decides not to follow me to the bathroom and instead ducks into the living room, where I hear him land with a soft thud on the couch.

It's taken some getting used to, being here in Rockford, though I think I like it. It's different from Milwaukee. There's less hustle here. Less stress. More open spaces. Less Mark. More Slater. The latter, I can very much get used to.

Of course, Slater would have moved to Milwaukee in a heartbeat. He was prepared to leave his job at the clinic and start fresh.

"I can find a job anywhere, Hannah," he told me. "You're the only place I want to be."

As if this dream life could have gotten any sweeter. But there was nothing left for me back there. Not a single thing—other than Maya, of course—worth staying for. Thankfully, my job made it easy to relocate. And so, here we are, in Slater's tiny bachelor apartment. He tells me we'll move into something nicer. "Just say the word, and we'll go"—anywhere I want. But there's something familiar about the intimate space here that leaves me feeling safe and content. I'm not sure I'm in a hurry to leave just yet.

The shower head turns on with a hiss as steam begins to rise, filling the room and softening the edges of the mirror. I undress, letting the sweet mix of exhaustion and satisfaction wash over me as I reflect on the long journey that brought me here. Moving the last of my things from Milwaukee has been exhausting over the past few months—though I have Maya to thank for most of it. She's been a true godsend. Without her, I would have had to face Mark far more than I ever wanted. It's because of her that I've even had the courage to take this leap and relocate with someone I've only known for six months. But, when it's real, you just know. At least, that's what she says. I'm truly lucky to have a friend like her on my side.

Steaming water hits my skin, and it's like a release—the water washing away the weight of my final trip to my old life. *You made it. You're finally on the other side.* The vision of my last and final suitcase sitting by the front door fills my heart with joy as I run my fingers through my damp hair. After so many painstakingly difficult months, my new chapter is about to begin, and I couldn't be more excited for what's to come.

The slow turn of the knob catches my attention with a faint click, interrupting my thoughts. I freeze, anticipating the voice I've been waiting to hear on the other side of the curtain.

"Isla?" His deep voice sends a shiver down my spine. "You're home."

"I am."

The word *home* lands in my chest like an anchor, grounding me, my heart swelling with love and the feeling of peace I've been longing for.

"I missed you." The urgency behind his words tells me he means it.

His silhouette moves in slow motion behind the curtain, his shirt slipping effortlessly over his head, landing softly on the bathroom floor. My breaths come fast and steady as I watch the form of his hands move to his waist, fingers working at the drawstring of his scrubs.

Slowly, the curtain peels back, and a rush of cold air sends a ripple of goosebumps trailing up my thighs. His forearm catches the light as he reaches in, his skin instantly soaked from the stream. Against his flexed muscle, I spot the gleam of fresh ink—a lone palm tree. My heart leaps. *He got it.*

A sly grin plays on his face as his eyes trace a slow path up and down my body. He shudders a thick, heavy breath that leaves me trembling for his touch.

"There's my girl."

Already my body aches for him, his deep, smoky tone like velvet to my soul as the hot water rolls down my body, trailing over my chilled skin.

"Tell me how much you missed me, baby."

"I missed you so much, Slater. I thought about you the whole time."

"I like hearing that." He steps closer, his scent filling the space, driving my senses wild as he tempts me with his words.

I reach out to touch him, my eager hands aching to pull him in here with me.

"Not so fast, Isla. Show me how you got on without me. Show me how you touched yourself when you thought about me."

My breath hitches, my cheeks burning scarlet at his request. For a moment, I freeze, unsure. The want—no, the need to please him surges through me, overwhelmingly strong, even though I've never done this before.

"Isla." There's a hint of warning in his voice, sharp and demanding as he watches.

I hold his gaze as my hand glides across my wet skin, grazing my nipples as I watch his longing expression. He climbs into the shower, one leg at a time, without breaking eye contact, the overspray already sticking in his stubble as he watches my hand slip between my slippery folds. A low groan escapes him as he moves closer, careful not to touch.

"Good girl, Isla."

His words are enough to undo me, my pulse pounding as my hips ache to close the distance between us. "I need you, Slater. Please."

"Not yet," he breathes, pressing his hands against the wall on either side of me.

A frustrated moan escapes my lips as I slide a finger into my arousal.

"That's it. Now tell me who you think about when you touch yourself like that, baby."

"You, Slater. Always you." I press my head back against the wall, savoring his every word.

"That's right. You're mine now. All mine, Isla. Every last inch of this tight little body. Finally."

"Yes, Slater. I'm all yours."

"Fuck right, you are."

Finally, he presses his body into mine, commanding my mouth with his as his tongue parts my lips, the water around us electric, sparking between us. I give in, letting his touch pull me apart, piece by trembling piece. With fingers tangled in my hair, he tilts my head to the side, whispering in my ear.

"Hands up, Isla, and take me like I know you can."

I shudder a breath as I reach my arms above my head, visions of the coconut grove replaying vividly in my mind—the sweet scent of fruit, ocean, sweat, and sun flooding my senses as my man fills every inch of me. Claiming me. Grounding me. Bringing me home.

THE END

About the Author

Cora Laine enjoys writing psychological thrillers with a touch of romance. She has a deep interest in the shadows people hide behind and is drawn to stories that blur the lines between truth and deception, love and obsession. Her debut novel, *A Familiar Lullaby*, is set to release soon. When not writing, Cora can usually be found scrolling bookstagram, sipping hot tea, or chasing chickens in the backyard. She's a firm believer in plot twists, quiet mornings spent at home, and the kind of characters that linger long after the last page.

Find Cora on Instagram, Facebook, TikTok & Bluesky at:
@coralaineauthor

Visit her website at:
www.coralaineauthor.com

Just One . . .

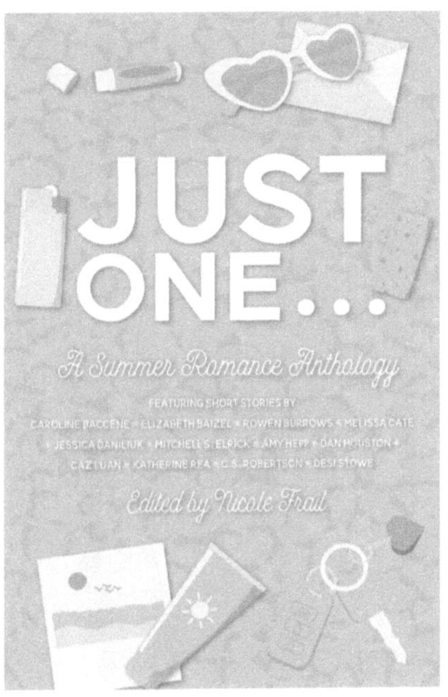

In this summer anthology, characters are denied the comfort of hiding the secrets or emotions they hold close when they are forced together as they travel to various locations.

Whether they involve the sharing of a bed or a car, or a tent on the trip of a lifetime, or something much smaller but necessary, these twelve stories are alive with tension as they highlight the challenge that is forced proximity.

Available in paperback & e-book.
Print ISBN: 978-1-965852-46-0
E-book ISBN: 978-1-965852-45-3

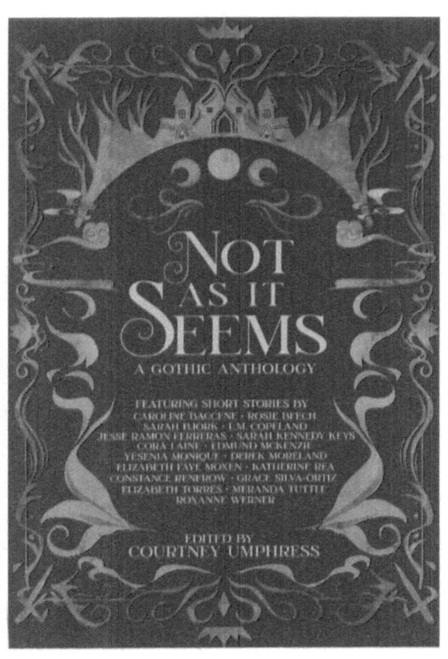

Not As It Seems

The unnerving short stories in this gothic anthology keep true intentions hidden and reality in check behind the seemingly normal perspective of the narrator. The characters take the reader to haunted seaside manors, mysterious towns, and grand homes shrouded in secrets as they explore the deceitful nature of the mind and how their pasts affect their futures.

These stories span genres, including thriller, horror, and fantasy—both historical and contemporary—and all ask the same question: Must you confront the horrors lurking in the shadows, or have they been a part of you all along?

Available in paperback & e-book.
Print ISBN: 978-1-965852-53-8
E-book ISBN: 978-1-965852-52-1

# A Familiar Lullaby

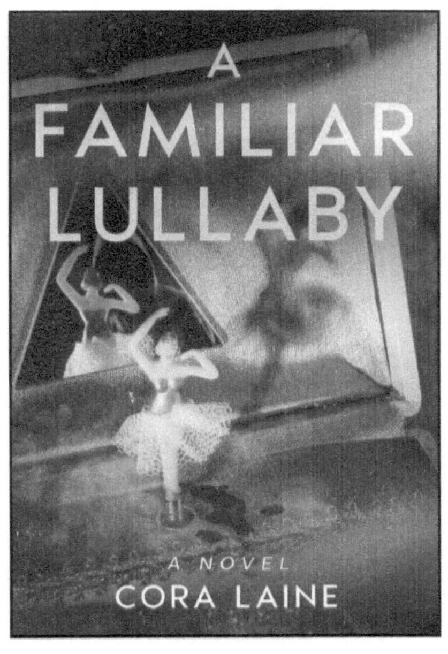

The country club community of Whispering Springs, lined with mansions, pocket dogs, and gossiping socialites—is no place for a girl from Trayer's Crossing, for a woman like Marin Allen with a haunted past she's managed to tuck away for more than a decade.

Now in her final year of law school, Marin fills her time wrapped tightly in the arms of esteemed finance advisor Tim Sullivan as they prepare for their upcoming wedding. Just as she finally accepts that she may have everything she's ever wanted, strange occurrences, shocking emails, and a series of violent and terrifying acts threatens to expose Marin's secrets and destroy the new life she's fought so hard for.

Can she stop the person behind it all before her new life burns to the ground?

Coming soon in paperback & e-book.

Attic Books and Attic Ebooks
are imprints of Nicole Frail Books, LLC,
an independent ("indie") publishing
company located in Avoca, Pennsylvania.

Attic Ebooks is a digital-first imprint and is
open to submissions of various lengths,
including short stories and essays and
novellas. If the length and market allows,
longer works are considered for print with
Attic Books.

To learn more about submitting a query to
Attic Ebooks, visit www.attic-ebooks.com.

Readers!
Join the NFB Street Team for exclusive first
reads and swag from Attic & Attic Ebooks!
www.nicolefrailbooks.com/street